THE
DRAG☾N
PRINCE

Callum's

~~Sketchbook~~

Spellbook

Photos © Shutterstock: cover texture (sergio34), 1 background and throughout
(Prakarn Pudtan), 6 top left background and throughout (Yevhenii Orlov), 12-13 center paper and throughout
(Karramba Production), 13 bottom right paper and throughout (autsawin uttisin), 14 paper and throughout
(DarkBird), 54-55 hands (Lemonade Serenade), 112-113 background wash and throughout (talloshau).

ISBN 978-1-338-62059-7

10 9 8 7 6 5 4 3 2 1   20 21 22 23 24

Printed in China 38
First printing 2020 • Book design by Betsy Peterschmidt and Christina Dacanay

THE DRAGON PRINCE

Callum's Spellbook

By Tracey West

SCHOLASTIC INC.

THIS BOOK BELONGS TO:

Callum

Dear Callum,

We don't know each other very well yet, but I can already see that you're a budding artist! I see you sketching on parchment with charcoal from the fireplace. I see you drawing in the dirt with sticks in the courtyard. I see you scratching artwork into the walls of your new bedroom with whatever you can find. :)

I don't really mind this castle gaining some new decoration "à la Callum," but I thought it was time you had a real sketchbook. I hope you'll fill it with not only your drawings but your dreams for the future, too, because I have a feeling you have great things inside you. And I can't wait to see you discover them.

With love,
Harrow

TABLE OF CONTENTS

How It All Started 8

Just the Five of Us 14

The Human World 38

The Kingdom of Katolis 40

My Family 42

Lord Viren and His Family 60

The Other Human Kingdoms 70

More People and Places in Katolis 74

Xadia 90

Elves of Xadia 94

Creatures of Xadia 114

Dragons of Xadia 118

Magic! 132

Primal Magic 134

Using Dark Magic 152

From Darkness to Light 156

So, this book started out as my sketchbook, after my stepdad gave it to me when I was a kid. I used to fill it with drawings of silly things, like marshmallow monsters.

But now I'm learning **MAGIC**, so this book is becoming less sketch-y and more spell-y, which I guess makes it a spellbook! Besides keeping track of all of the incantations and other mage things I'm learning, I also think it's important to write down everything that's happening right now. Because big things are happening — BIG things — things that people are going to talk about hundreds of years from now. I want to get all the details right. Every person. Every place. Every battle.

I'll still sketch some silly things once in a while — Ezran would be disappointed if I stopped! (He's always leafing through my sketchbook.) My friends peek at it sometimes, too. Hey! If you're reading this, I guess you're also my friend. At least, I hope you're a friend . . . I wouldn't want my enemies reading this, that's for sure!

-Callum

How It All Started

My whole life, the world has been split into two parts: the <u>human world</u>, which is made up of five kingdoms, and <u>Xadia</u>, a magical land filled with elves and dragons and all kinds of other amazing creatures. When I was little, I asked my mom why we could never go to Xadia, and she told me a story:

Long ago, there were six primal sources of magic in the world: the Sun, the Moon, the Stars, the Earth, the Sky, and the Ocean.

Elves and dragons were born connected to the primal sources; humans weren't. But a human mage discovered a seventh source: dark magic.

Mom didn't like talking about dark magic. She told me it's complicated because with dark magic, there's always a cost. To perform dark magic, you have to obtain the essence of a magical creature, and there are only a couple ways of doing that — by stealing it, such as cutting off a dragon's or unicorn's horn, or the more common way: by killing the creature.

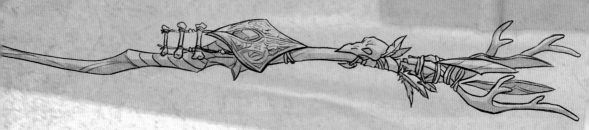

Mom's story continued:

The elves and dragons were horrified by the humans' use of dark magic. To punish the humans, they banished them to the western part of the continent.

For hundreds of years after that, the Dragon King, Thunder, defended the border between the two worlds.

And that's where my mom's story ends, but sort of where my story starts? Because everything in this book stems from what happened next: My mom died during a battle with the Dragon King, and to get revenge, King Harrow (my stepdad) and Lord Viren killed Thunder and destroyed his egg. Or at least, that's what everybody thought.

Xadia decided to seek revenge for the death of Thunder (I'm sensing a pattern here . . .). That's when Ezran and I met Rayla — an elf! And then we discovered that the dragon egg wasn't destroyed — Lord Viren had been hiding it!

This was our chance. We decided to return the dragon egg to its mother in Xadia. It hasn't been an easy journey so far, but it's our only hope for restoring peace.

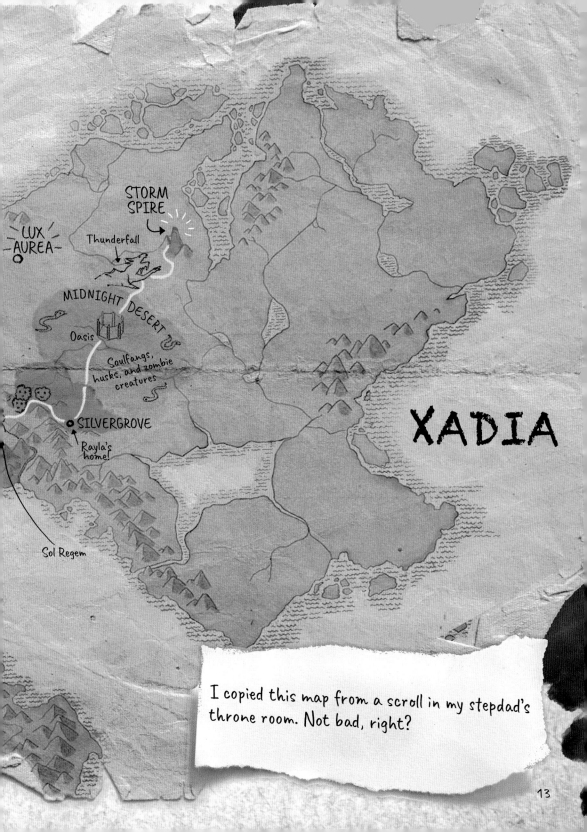

STORM
SPIRE

Thunderfall

LUX
AUREA

MIDNIGHT DESERT

Oasis

Soulfangs,
husks, and zombie
creatures

SILVERGROVE

Rayla's
home!

Sol Regem

XADIA

I copied this map from a scroll in my stepdad's
throne room. Not bad, right?

Just the Five of Us

This whole journey has been really intense and amazing, and I've met so many new people and magical creatures along the way. But through it all, it's been the five of us: me, Ezran, Rayla, Bait, and Zym. (Although in the beginning, Zym was silent, hard, and round — because he was an egg!)

It took me a few years to get good at drawing. Maybe it will be like that with magic, too.

ME (CALLUM)

Officially I'm Prince Callum, because my mom was queen of Katolis. I never really felt like a prince, though. But that's okay — now I know I was always meant to be a <u>mage</u>.

ROLE: Big brother; mage-in-training

STRENGTHS AND SPECIAL SKILLS: I'm supposed to be good at prince stuff like sword fighting and riding horses. Sword fighting is NOT my thing!

But what I'm really good at is drawing and doing magic.

ACCESSORIES: Sketchbook; Rune Cube; Katolis scarf

LIKES: Dusty old books; the rain; made-up words (such as "breakfunch," which is much funner to say than just "brunch")

DISLIKES: Posing too long for official portraits; finding jelly tart crumbs in my bed that didn't come from me

My little brother's jelly tart obsession is out of control. He gets it from our mom.

EZRAN

I used to think my little brother was just a cute kid who liked to play hide-and-seek and eat jelly tarts. It was hard to imagine him being king someday. But now I've seen how brave and wise he can be. If anybody deserves the throne, it's him.

ROLE: Protector of the Dragon Prince; rightful King of Katolis

STRENGTHS AND SPECIAL SKILLS: Ezran can communicate with animals.

ACCESSORIES: He never goes anywhere without his backpack.

LIKES: Hide-and-go-seek; other games with friends and pets; jelly tarts! And, of course, Bait and Zym. And any other creatures he meets.

DISLIKES: War; fighting; cruelty; excessively mushy peas

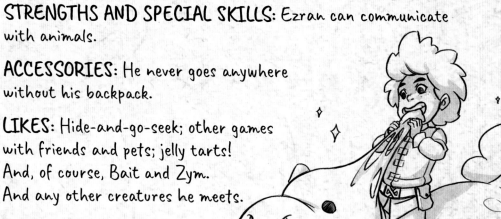

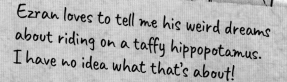

Ezran loves to tell me his weird dreams about riding on a taffy hippopotamus. I have no idea what that's about!

How Ezran
~~TALKS TO~~ ANIMALS
Communicates with!

Callum asked me
to tell him how I
talk to animals.
I told him I don't
~~talk~~ to animals!
Not really. Then
I made him give
me his book so I
could make sure
he got it right.

It's always been hard for me to make
friends with other kids. I just feel
like I don't fit in. But with
animals, it's different. I
have a connection with
them. A few years ago,
I realized I could
understand what they
were saying.

It's not like I hear words in my head. I just try to think really hard about how they're feeling, and then I try to feel the same way. And I try to understand. So it's like I can feel what they want me to know . . . It's hard to explain. But they understand me the same way.

Callum didn't believe me at first. Once he asked me to prove it to him, so I communicated with some raccoons. They told me to look for treasure under a waterfall. Callum and I looked, but it wasn't there. Callum said it proved I was lying. But the raccoons were playing a trick on me. Since then, I never trust raccoons! (Although they are so cute, with their little masks.)

—Ez

I will never doubt you again, Ez, I promise! —Callum

OH, BROTHER!

Ez and I have an agreement: If I do something a big brother shouldn't do (like not believe him about the animals), I have to do "Callum's Famous Jerkface Dance." It always makes him smile!

How bright can Bait flash? Bright enough to blind his enemies when they're not suspecting it! Bait's flash has saved us a bunch of times.

BAIT

Nobody knows how old Bait is, exactly. He was King Harrow's pet before he became Ezran's. Technically, he's a chroma-luminescent amphibian, but most people call him a glow toad. A **GRUMPY** glow toad.

ROLE: Loyal protector of Ezran; glow warrior

STRENGTHS AND SPECIAL SKILLS: He changes colors depending on his mood. And he can flash REALLY bright (but only when he feels like it).

LIKES: Ezran, and jelly tarts. Oh, and he secretly loves belly rubs!

DISLIKES: Almost everything else. But he especially dislikes when Ezran pays attention to Zym instead of him. He gets so jealous!

The reason Bait is called Bait is kind of funny — unless you're Bait, I guess. Apparently, glow toads are delicious! Fishermen use them as bait to catch big fish, so . . . Bait! Ezran says Bait doesn't know he's delicious, but I think that might be why he's grumpy all the time.

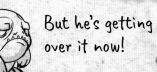

But he's getting over it now!

The MANY COLORS of BAIT

Bait is patient and never lashes out unless he's in danger, but you can tell what kind of mood he's in by paying attention to his colors.

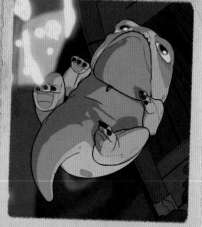

YELLOW:
This is regular grumpy Bait.

BLUE: Sleepy and grumpy.

RED: Angry and grumpy. When you see red, stay away!

GRAY: Sad and grumpy. Bait turns gray when he can't be with Ezran. He also turns gray when he's sick.

GREEN: Jealous and grumpy. When Ezran pays a lot of attention to Zym, Bait turns green. I've also seen him turn bright green when he's really afraid — like when we were climbing up the Cursed Caldera.

PINK: Embarrassed and grumpy. One time, when I said I thought a sign was for a dating service for pets, he turned bright pink!

PURPLE: Stressed and grumpy — like when the baker squeezes him in a super-tight hug!

ORANGE: He turns this color when he's feeling especially loved (and grumpy). I saw him turn orange when Rayla told him that he was her hero.

BONUS BAIT: When he drinks moonberry juice, he glows bright red and blue!

27

Other than her amazing fighting skills, there are many ways you can tell that Rayla is a Moonshadow elf:

Her horns

Cool blue markings

White hair

Moon shapes on her belt

Four fingers

RAYLA

I never thought I'd be friends with an elf, but I'm sure glad she's on our side. Rayla is good, fearless, and strong. She's also a back-flipping, tree-climbing, sword-swinging warrior!

ROLE: Moonshadow elf assassin

STRENGTHS AND SPECIAL SKILLS: Incredibly quick on her feet; can transform into Moonshadow form

WEAPONS AND ACCESSORIES: Butterfly blades; assassin's binding

LIKES: Sarcasm; making fun of how humans talk; adoraburrs; Moonberry Surprise

DISLIKES: Lujanne's kooky wisdom. And water! She's scared of it!

Moonshadow elf assassins literally bind themselves to their missions through a magic ritual. The ribbon tightens gradually while the target is still alive, only falling off once the mission is complete.

Rayla's team was charged with killing King Harrow and Ezran, but Rayla refused to kill Ezran. When I realized she was willing to lose her hand to protect him, I knew I could really trust her.

Rayla's BUTTERFLY BLADES

Because the blades have many different configurations, Rayla can use them for more than just fighting, like for climbing or for wedging things apart.

I **think** this is how her blades go from closed to open. It's hard to tell because she always does it so fast!

My stepdad always told me that weapons made with elven craftsmanship were the best in the world. I didn't know what he meant until I saw Rayla use her butterfly blades. It's amazing to watch her use them — it's like they're an extension of her two hands! Once I asked if I could try them and she told me no, that I'd probably end up hurting myself. I think she had a point.

Haha! Point.
Get it?

"HUMAN" RAYLA

Callum's been writing a lot about me in his book, but he left out one of my very best skills: pretending to be human!

It's easy! All I need is a hood to cover my horns and gloves to hide the fact that I have four fingers instead of five. (Who needs a pinky, anyway? Doesn't it just get in the way?)

Once I've got my disguise, I just add my perfect human impression. I say lots of things humans might say, like:

"I sure do like talking about money, don't you?"

"Hey, let's start a war!"

"I enjoy staying out in the sun even though I know it's bad for me!"

"Let's go judge and criticize things other humans do, and then do the exact same things ourselves!"

"I am excited to rapidly eat a plate of unwholesome food in an excessive portion size!"

"Other human, let's talk about which roads and pathways will take us somewhere slightly faster than other roads and pathways!"

"My, your skull is very smooth!"

"I love saying 'I know, right?' to tell someone I agree with them."

If Rayla can impersonate a human, then I can impersonate an elf!

"Oi! I'm an Earthblood elf! All me best friends are trees!"

33

The STORY of the EGG

When we first started our journey, it was just four of us — me, Ezran, Rayla, and Bait — and one dragon egg. I'll never forget the moment I saw that egg. Everyone had said the heir to the Dragon King had been destroyed, but Ezran discovered the egg hidden in Viren's chambers! "This changes everything," Rayla said when we found the egg. She was right. We knew we had to return the egg to its mother to stop the war brewing between the human world and Xadia.

Ezran made a connection with the egg right away, and kept it in his backpack whenever he could.

Early in our journey to Xadia, we got caught in an avalanche and ended up on an icy pond. I tried to pass the egg to Rayla to keep it safe, but her bad hand couldn't hold it, and it fell into the freezing water. Before we could stop him, Ez dove in to save the egg!

The egg wasn't the same after that. In fact, for a terrifying moment, we thought it died.

The Moon mage Lujanne told us the Dragon Prince would definitely die if the egg didn't hatch soon, and that because the Dragon Prince is a Sky dragon, he would only hatch in the eye of a storm. So I broke my **PRIMAL STONE** to release the storm inside. Lightning struck the egg, it cracked open . . . and out hatched the most adorable baby dragon you could ever imagine!

More on the primal stone later!

AZYMONDIAS

That's his fancy Dragon Prince name — we just call him Zym. Even though Zym will be the most powerful being in the world someday, right now he's like a playful puppy. He's really curious about the world around him.

ROLE: Dragon Prince of Xadia

STRENGTHS AND SPECIAL SKILLS: He can shoot off sparks, but he can't control them yet. He's also incredibly cute!

LIKES: Running in circles; sniffing flowers; napping with Ezran

DISLIKES: Heights, but he seems to be getting a little braver every day

Zym has a big appetite!

Ez has been working hard to help Zym learn how to fly. Soren made a "slidey-sling-go-fast-rope" for them to train on, but Rayla put a stop to that when she figured out how dangerous it was!

The HUMAN WORLD

It's kind of funny to call where I grew up "the human world," because back then, it was the only world I ever knew. There are five kingdoms in all, and my stepdad, King Harrow, ruled the kingdom of Katolis.

Rayla says that in Xadia, all of the elves are taught that humans are evil, but now she knows that's not true. The five kingdoms are filled with all kinds of people — some good, some bad, and some in-between. I'm going to write about the ones who are important to our story — and some important places, too.

NEOLANDIA

DUREN

DEL BAR

KATOLIS

EVENERE

THE KINGDOM

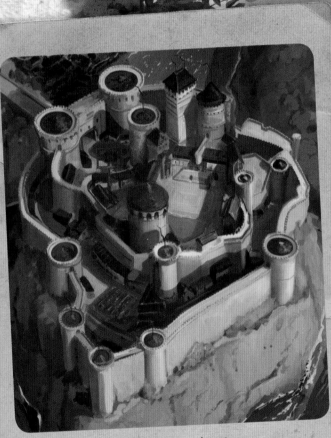

Katolis Castle is enormous! When my mom and I moved in when I was a little kid, I used to get lost all the time.

OF KATOLIS

Not everyone in Katolis lives in the castle. We have villagers, shopkeepers, farmers, teachers, artists — all kinds of people!

Don't forget bakers!
— Ez

First up —
MY FAMILY!

My stepdad really loved Pip, his pet Xadian songbird. He became really attached to Pip after my mom died.

King Harrow always looked serious in his portraits, but in person he was really funny. I know I'll miss his jokes — even if they were awful!

KING HARROW

My mom married King Harrow when I was a kid, so he's my stepdad. For years, I thought of him as the king instead of my dad. But after I lost him, I realized that he'd been a great father to me all along.

ROLE: King of Katolis

STRENGTHS/SPECIAL SKILLS: He was a great warrior, and a just and fair king who always tried to do the right thing for his people. But some of the decisions he made led us to the brink of war with Xadia.

WEAPONS/ACCESSORIES: His crown; his sword

LIKED: Justice; family; sledding; lightly teasing Bait; telling dad jokes

DISLIKED: Unfairness; inequality; "crown hair" (a little indent from when you wear your crown too long)

No matter how busy he was, my stepdad always had time for me. In the summer, we would go down to the river to cool off.

A LIE, A WISH, AND A SECRET

Before he died, King Harrow wrote me a letter. I didn't want to read it right away. The letter was all I had left of him, and I knew that when I finished reading it, his death would feel final.

I'm glad I finally read it. He gave me a lot to think about. In the letter, he said he had to tell me a lie, a wish, and a secret.

First came the lie: that being vulnerable and kind made you weak. He told me that true strength is found in love.

Next came the wish: for me and Ezran to be free. He said that our future doesn't have to be based on our past. I think he means a lot of things when he says that — but mainly that we don't have to seek revenge for his death. Or for what happened to my mom. That's a big deal, because it means we can break this cycle of revenge between the humans and Xadia.

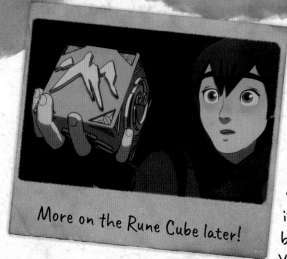

More on the Rune Cube later!

Finally came the secret, and it was a good one: He told me there was a magical cube at the Banther Lodge. It has runes carved into it and glows when it's near something magical. He said it was an ancient relic that belonged to an elven wizard in Xadia named Aaravos. It's called the Key of Aaravos, which is strange because it's shaped like a cube. Maybe it unlocks something really important?

I have no idea what the key is for, or how to find that out. But an even bigger question is: Why did my stepdad want _me_ to have the cube? Why not Lord Viren, who's an expert mage? Or someone he trusts in the castle, like Opeli? Why _me_?

I like to think it's because he saw something in me — something I didn't even see in myself. He gave me this notebook all those years ago, and now it's become my spellbook. Maybe he knew I was a mage even before I did.

I am smiling so big as I write this, thinking about King Harrow. Once Zym is safely back with his mom, I will find out what the Key of Aaravos does. I will make ~~King Harrow~~ Dad proud.

Inside
KATOLIS CASTLE

Living in the castle was a lot more comfy than sleeping on the ground all the time, like we do now. Ez and I used to share a room. I had my own desk where I could do my sketching.

The SYMBOL OF KATOLIS is a castle with two uneven towers. You can see it in our banner, on the king's crown, on the weaponry, and even on the scarf that I always wear. When I was little, my stepdad told me the symbol has to do with what's special about humans. That it's about finding strength in our differences.

The room Ez misses most in the castle is the kitchen. He loved trying to sneak jelly tarts from BARIUS THE BAKER. Barius usually gave Ez one tart, scolded him, and sent him on his way. But I think his heart is as soft as a sticky bun. One time, I caught him feeding tarts to Bait!

Crows send messages from our castle to the other kingdoms. Usually the Crow Lord is in charge of that, but now the CROW MASTER fills in when needed. He's sort of like an assistant Crow Lord. He recently got promoted and he's pretty proud of it!

I will never forget Mom's face. And I'll always remember her laugh. How her breath smelled of persimmons. And how when she and my stepdad practiced sword fighting, she always beat him!

MY MOM, SARAI

I know that she died bravely, doing what she thought was the right thing. But I don't really like to think about her dying. I'd rather think about her when she was alive.

ROLE: Queen of Katolis

STRENGTHS/SPECIAL SKILLS: She was a skilled horseback rider and a warrior. She gave amazing hugs. And I'm pretty sure Ez gets his big heart from her (and I guess I do, too!).

WEAPONS/ACCESSORIES: Her crown; her spear

LIKED: Me and Ez; my stepdad's corny jokes; sweets (even more than Ezran does!); her little sister, Amaya

DISLIKED: Anyone eating the last jelly tart; anyone telling her she couldn't do something; boring dreams

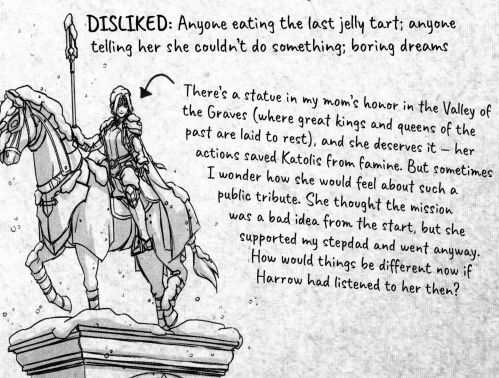

There's a statue in my mom's honor in the Valley of the Graves (where great kings and queens of the past are laid to rest), and she deserves it — her actions saved Katolis from famine. But sometimes I wonder how she would feel about such a public tribute. She thought the mission was a bad idea from the start, but she supported my stepdad and went anyway. How would things be different now if Harrow had listened to her then?

THE BANTHER LODGE

We used to go here every winter as a family to play in the snow and go sledding. When Rayla, Ez, and I started out on our journey, I remembered seeing a cube thing with magical symbols on it in the game room when I was a kid. I thought the cube might help us out, so I convinced Rayla that we should stop by the Banther Lodge on the way to Xadia.

But before I found the cube, Aunt Amaya found us, and boy, was she happy to see us alive! She knew assassins had come to the castle, and that we were in danger. Ez wanted to tell her that we had found the dragon egg and were traveling with Rayla to return it to Xadia, but I didn't think she would understand. When we got in a sticky situation, I told her that Rayla was a bloodthirsty elf who had kidnapped us — I hoped it would allow us to escape together. The lie let us continue on our journey, but Rayla still hasn't fully forgiven me for it.

The lodge may be where I found the cube, but I'll always remember it as the place where we had fun as a family. My stepdad always loved it when we went really fast!

I've seen Aunt Amaya use her shield for more than just defense. Both the top and bottom are super sharp, so she can use the shield as an attack weapon, too.

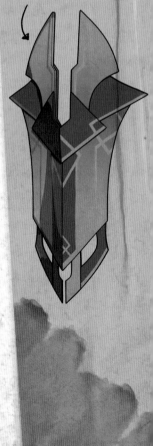

AUNT AMAYA

Aunt Amaya is my mom's sister, and they were a lot alike. She is a brave warrior, like my mom was. She's a trusted general, too. But while my mom could hear, Aunt Amaya was born deaf. That didn't stop her from becoming one of the strongest soldiers in Katolis. In fact, my mom told me that Aunt Amaya's difference is part of why she has a stronger awareness and strategic sense than any other general!

ROLE: General in the Army of Katolis

STRENGTHS/SPECIAL SKILLS: One of the most physically powerful soldiers in the army; a skilled sword fighter; speaks sign language. She's an inspiring leader, too, and her troops are stronger knowing she's in charge.

WEAPONS/ACCESSORIES: Sword; shield; armor

LIKES: A good fight; breakfast; her nephews

DISLIKES: Liars; skipping meals; salads; ~~elves~~

I am strong enough to admit mistakes, and I was WRONG to think all elves are bad! In fact, some are rather good . . .

—Love, Aunt Amaya

Aunt Amaya wasn't always around when we were growing up because she and her troops guard the Breach, an important part of the border between the human kingdoms and Xadia. But whenever she visited the castle, she always made time for us.

SIGN LANGUAGE

Aunt Amaya taught me some sign language when I was little, and Ez asked me to teach him some, too. The easiest thing to learn is the alphabet.

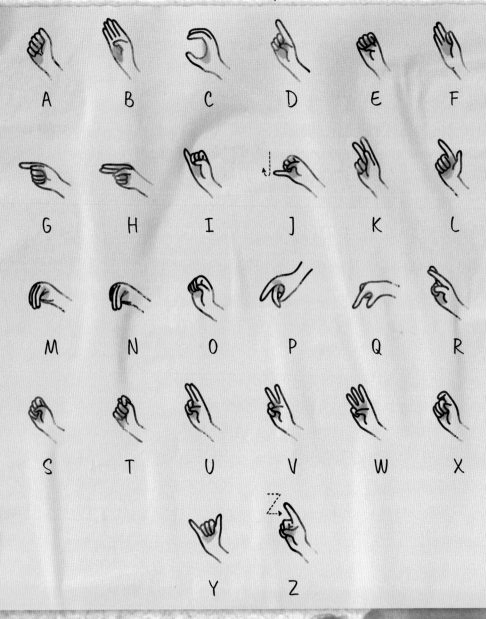

Hey Ez — here's some practice for you! Can you figure out this secret Aunt Amaya always told me when we were little?

I think I got it! That is very true. — Ez

Gren and Opeli aren't family — but our family wouldn't be complete without them!

COMMANDER GREN

He is almost always by Aunt Amaya's side, and not just because he's her sign language interpreter. He is her loyal and trusted second-in-command. No matter how bad things get, Gren is always sunny and optimistic.

ROLE: General Amaya's second-in-command and interpreter

STRENGTHS/SPECIAL SKILLS: Hard working and honest; speaks sign language

WEAPONS/ACCESSORIES: Shoulder armor; wrist gauntlets; does not carry a weapon

LIKES: Strawberry shortcake; Amaya; Corvus; peace and quiet; noodle dishes

DISLIKES: : Loud noises; mustard; "can't do" attitudes; frowns that have not yet been turned upside down

HIGH CLERIC OPELI

She has been an adviser to King Harrow ever since I can remember. My stepdad always trusted her to give him good advice. She's the only one I've ever seen stand up to Lord Viren. In fact, she seems to enjoy it.

ROLE: Cleric of the Katolis High Council

STRENGTHS/SPECIAL SKILLS: She knows every rule and law of the kingdom by heart.

ACCESSORIES: Hooded cloak; silver headband

LIKES: Traditions; holidays; planning parties; the beach

DISLIKES: Messes; rule breakers; laziness; too many people in the throne room

When Ezran decided to return to Katolis after we learned of King Harrow's death, I was really glad Corvus agreed to accompany him. Although I don't think Corvus was too happy that they hitched a ride on two banthers!

CORVUS

Even though Corvus has been part of Aunt Amaya's crew for a long time, I didn't know who he was until she sent him to track us. Rayla says he's got better tracking skills than a Moonshadow elf, and that's a BIG compliment.

ROLE: General Amaya's top tracker — she sends him out on lots of secret missions

STRENGTHS/SPECIAL SKILLS: Besides being an expert tracker, he is athletic and loyal. He has a dry sense of humor, too. When I told him I have a "wet" sense of humor, he nodded but he did not laugh.

WEAPONS/ACCESSORIES: Grappling hook; earth-colored clothes that help him blend into the forest

LIKES: Horses; a well-tied knot; camping; winning scavenger hunts

DISLIKES: Paperwork; being cooped up indoors; riddles; chains or ropes that get tangled

Corvus swings the hook on the end of the chain, and then launches it at opponents to capture them or yank their weapons from them. Once I asked Corvus if his enemies really believe that crazy thing is his weapon, or if they think he's "yanking their chain." He nodded and smiled that time, but he did not laugh.

When my mom and I first came to the castle, I didn't know anybody. Lord Viren and his children, Claudia and Soren, were kind of like my second family.

The Viren I remember was a kind dad who loved his kids. He's a different man now.

LORD VIREN

When I first met Lord Viren, he was my stepdad's best friend. Then after my mom died, he started doing more and more dark magic to help the kingdom, but I think it only made things worse. And now it looks like dark magic has poisoned his soul.

ROLE: High Mage of the Kingdom of Katolis

STRENGTHS/SPECIAL SKILLS: He is a master at dark magic; in the past, he used it to help the kingdom. Now, I think he only wants power for himself.

WEAPONS/ACCESSORIES: His staff was made by elves, and I've seen him use it to perform dark magic.

LIKES: King Harrow; his children; being appreciated; dark magic; problem-solving; puzzles; hot brown morning potion; strong cheese

DISLIKES: Showing weakness; Opeli; seagulls; weak cheese; anyone who disagrees or can't keep up with him

The night Ez and I left the castle, Lord Viren put a dark magic spell on me so that I couldn't talk to my stepdad. The look in his eyes was . . . pure evil.

Claudia loves reading more than anybody I know. She even reads while she walks! Once I saw her walk into a tree because she had her nose buried in a book.

CLAUDIA

Claudia was one of my closest friends growing up, but now I feel like I don't know who she is. I hate to imagine that she's as evil as her father, but she seems to be loyal to him and his cause. I know she has a good heart, so maybe she'll end up doing the right thing?

ROLE: Mage-in-training; sent on a mission to retrieve the dragon egg from us

STRENGTHS/SPECIAL SKILLS: She's really good at magic

WEAPONS/ACCESSORIES: Her satchel, which is filled with ingredients for doing dark magic; her book of spells

LIKES: Her family (she loves Soren and Viren a lot!); ancient ruins; cute things; hot brown morning potion

DISLIKES: Lukewarm brown morning potion

When Claudia first learned dark magic, she did fun things with it, like prank Soren and make extra-fluffy pancakes. She even invented "hot brown morning potion," which helped her perk up after a long night of reading.

Dear Claudia,

I know we've been friends for a long time. But lately, I've been feeling this . . . spark between us (and not just when you make actual sparks with your magic — ha ha!).

I've been meaning to tell you how much I love how much you love magic. Err . . . that was confusing. What I mean is, you light up when you do magic, or even just talk about it. I'd really like to learn some spells from you. Maybe you could give me a lesson sometime?

If you don't want to give me a magic lesson, that's fine, but maybe we could still, you know, hang out? You know, like, just you and me? We could drink some hot brown morning potion and just, you know, talk.

Anyway . . . I hope you like this drawing
I did of us. I'll talk to you soon? Maybe?

Yours,

Callum

I wrote this letter to Claudia, but I wasn't brave enough to give it to her. I pasted it into my sketchbook and forgot about it. Now . . . I'm glad I didn't. I don't feel the same way anymore. Maybe because Claudia's not the same person I once knew.

I hope I'm one-tenth the mage Claudia is someday. Or maybe an eighth if I work hard at it!

I mean, what's not to love about this face? Sigh. I miss silly Claudia!

Soren doesn't understand Claudia's obsession with magic and magical creatures. To him, a good old-fashioned sword fight is the best way to solve a problem!

SOREN

Claudia might be a lot like her dad, but Soren doesn't remind me of Lord Viren at all. He's outgoing and loud and really goofy sometimes. Growing up, he always teased me for being weak and called me names like "step-prince." But he always made me laugh.

ROLE: Member of the Crownguard of Katolis (the youngest one ever!); sent on a mission to retrieve the dragon egg from us (and get rid of me and Ez for good!)

STRENGTHS/SPECIAL SKILLS: Sword fighting; horseback riding — all the things I was supposed to be good at as a prince, but wasn't

WEAPONS/ ACCESSORIES: Armor; cape; sword

LIKES: Pancakes; butter; his muscles

DISLIKES: The moon; moths; magic (especially when it involves something weird or gross)

Soren definitely bullied me sometimes, but he could also be unexpectedly nice — like when he let me pretend to win a sword fight so I could impress Claudia.

HEY STEP-PRINCE!

I KNOW YOU HAVE YOUR NOSE IN THIS BOOK ALL DAY, SO I'M GOING TO LEAVE YOU SOME WORKOUT TIPS IN HERE. IF YOU'RE GOING TO BE A REAL PRINCE SOMEDAY, YOU NEED TO GET THOSE MEASLY MUSCLES OF YOURS IN SHAPE!

BEFORE ANY WORKOUT, MAKE SURE YOU STRETCH!

CLIMBING UP THE CASTLE STEPS IS GREAT FOR YOUR LEG MUSCLES.

OFFICIAL MEETINGS ARE JUST A LOT OF TALKING. GET SOME SQUATS IN WHILE EVERYONE ELSE IS BLABBING.

DO ALL THIS EVERY DAY AND PRETTY SOON YOU'LL BE ABLE TO LIFT MORE THAN YOUR PENCIL! (GET IT? BECAUSE YOU'RE ALWAYS SKETCHING.)

—SOREN

Sure, I'll get to this, Soren.
Right after I'm done with these drawings . . .

The OTHER HUMAN KINGDOMS

Besides Katolis, there are four other human kingdoms. They all have a say in whether or not the humans will wage war on Xadia. Some of them have a lot more to say than others!

EVENERE

RULER: Queen Fareeda

SYMBOL: Dragonfly

I've never met Queen Fareeda. In fact, most people haven't — Evenere is an island kingdom far to the west and you can only get there by boat. I've heard it's really swampy so you'd think the people there would be kind of dreary, but my stepdad always said Queen Fareeda was cheery and bright.

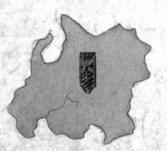

NEOLANDIA

RULERS: King Ahling, Prince Kasef

SYMBOL: Elephant

I met Prince Kasef when I was a kid, and he reminded me of Soren — tall and strong and good at everything. Now I know that he's nothing like Soren, really. He's filled with anger and hatred for things he doesn't understand.

DUREN

RULER: Queen Aanya

SYMBOL: Flower

Queen Aanya was practically a baby when she inherited the throne after both her mothers died. A lot of enemies came after her, but she defeated them. She became a really smart ruler as a result. I know what it's like to lose both parents, so Aanya must be made of pretty tough stuff.

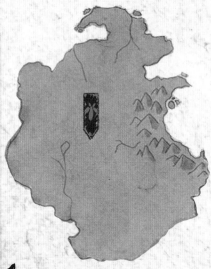

Queen Annika and Queen Neha asked for help from Katolis when a famine struck Duren. They died trying to take the heart of the magma titan to save both kingdoms (the same mission that killed my mom).

DEL BAR

RULER: King Florian

SYMBOL: Dragon

The few times I've met King Florian, he acted like everyone's uncle. He never stopped laughing or patting everyone on the back really hard. My stepdad pretended it didn't hurt, but it definitely did. I guess you have to be pretty strong and upbeat when you lead a kingdom so far up in the freezing mountains!

As we headed toward Xadia, we traveled to **PLACES IN KATOLIS** I'd never been before, and met some **NEW FRIENDS** along the way. This notebook wouldn't be complete without them!

ELLIS

Ellis is pretty amazing. I mean, what kid rides around on a wolf? It's a good thing we found her, because without her, our journey would have ended in her little mountain town.

ROLE: She led us to the top of the Cursed Caldera to help us find a healer for the dragon egg.

STRENGTHS/SPECIAL SKILLS: She has a caring heart, and she's brave. Not many kids would rescue an injured wolf pup they found in the woods.

ACCESSORIES: When you live in the snowy mountains, you gotta wear a fur hat!

LIKES: Her pet wolf, Ava; hanging around with Ezran

DISLIKES: Anyone who harms animals

AVA

When Ellis found Ava, the wolf had lost one of her legs in a trap. Ellis's family wouldn't let her keep a three-legged pup, so Ellis ran away with Ava. They were traveling up the Cursed Caldera when a mysterious healer found them. The healer regrew Ava's leg — or that's what Ellis thought, anyway. It turns out that the magic charm around Ava's neck makes it look like she has four legs — but she still only has three. Ava gets around just fine on three legs. It's the rest of the world that thinks she needs four!

75

THE CURSED

Why is this place cursed? Locals say that it's inhabited by scary creatures. The higher you climb, the more terrifying the creatures become!

Sir Phinneas

The Great Explorer

Rayla thought maybe the mountain was named after the famous explorer, Sir Phineas Kirst. There are pictures of him in the history books in the castle. But this mountain is a totally different kind of <u>cursed.</u>

CALDERA

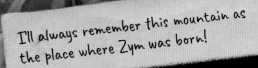

It didn't take long before we ran into monsters. The first one was this giant leech. Gross! But thanks to Ez, we learned that the monsters weren't real — they were illusions created by a Moon mage.

Lujanne's best friend is Phoe-Phoe (pronounced fee-fee), a Xadian Moon phoenix. She's strongest when she's close to the Moon Nexus. It could be dangerous for her to fly too far away from it.

LUJANNE

Lujanne is the Moon mage who lives on the top of the Cursed Caldera. She creates the monster illusions to protect the Moon Nexus, a powerful center of Moon magic that the elves used before the world was split in two. Even though Lujanne didn't turn out to be a healer, she knew what we needed to do to get Zym to hatch. And she taught me a lot about Moon magic.

ROLE: Guardian of the Moon Nexus

STRENGTHS/SPECIAL SKILLS: She is a master of illusion — she can feed you worms and make you think you're eating delicious cake!

ACCESSORIES: Cape with moon symbols

LIKES: Having fun with humans who get too close to the Nexus by melting their minds with illusions. "They would completely freak your bean," she told me.

DISLIKES: Living alone on a mountain for decades can get lonely, even if you do have a magical bird for company.

When she's not scaring off trespassing humans, Lujanne's got to do <u>something</u> to pass the time. There is no more devious opponent for Lujanne than herself!

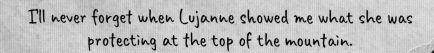

The MOON NEXUS

I'll never forget when Lujanne showed me what she was
protecting at the top of the mountain.

I'll always remember
the Moon Nexus,
because it's where
Claudia told me that
King Harrow had died.

and the MOONHENGE

This is the **MOONHENGE**. A long time ago, when Xadia was one land, Moonshadow elves performed fantastic rituals here. Now it's in ruins. The Moon Druids destroyed it themselves when Xadia was divided in two. Ever since then, there's always been a Guardian of the Moon Nexus to prevent humans from discovering it.

A place where the magic of a primal energy is at its most pure and powerful is called a <u>Nexus</u>. The **MOON NEXUS** reflects the moon perfectly. When the moon is full, its light completely fills the lake. Legends say that ancient elves could use the power of the Nexus to open up a portal to another plane — a shimmering world between life and death. I wonder if that's true?

What to Eat
WHEN YOU'RE ON THE RUN

So, the big problem with being on the run is that there isn't a nice, warm kitchen you can go to where someone will give you tasty food. On this journey we've eaten rock-hard bread, moonberries, and . . . worms. Lots of worms. More worms than a person should eat. Which is any number above zero.

We stocked up on some old bread at the Banther Lodge. But it was so hard I'm amazed we didn't break our teeth eating it!

When Rayla first offered us moonberry juice, I thought it was, well, blood. Until that point, I thought elves were all bloodthirsty fiends — but I know different now. Moonberry juice is really delicious. It's too bad Bait drank it all!

Lujanne put an illusion on worms so that we would think we were eating delicious food. But once you learn the truth, the magic disappears.

When Ezran came back from the castle, he gave me this — the recipe for jelly tarts from Barius the baker. Maybe one day, when this is all over, we can make some together.

JELLY TARTS

Barius says to make sure you always have an adult help you with the oven! — Ez

Ingredients:

1½ cups flour

½ cup sugar

¼ teaspoon salt

½ cup softened butter

3 ounces softened cream cheese

3 tablespoons cold water

½ cup jam or jelly (any kind, but Prince — I mean King Ezran likes strawberry best)

1. In a bowl, stir up the flour, sugar, and salt. Then add the butter and cream cheese. Beat it as fast as you can until it's nice and crumbly. Then add the water and keep beating until it turns into a smooth dough.

2. Take your dough ball and divide it into two pieces. Flatten each piece and wrap it in a clear wrap. Put it somewhere nice and cold for about 3 hours.

3. Get your oven nice and hot — 375 degrees Fahrenheit.

4. Sprinkle some flour on your table and roll out the dough so it's about ⅛ of an inch thick. Then cut circles out of the dough. The circles should be about 2½ inches wide. Using a cookie cutter — or even a glass turned upside down — works! Place your dough circles on a baking sheet.

5. Put ½ teaspoon of jelly into the center of each circle. Lift up the edges and pinch them together at three points to form triangles. Pinch them very tightly so they don't let the jelly out when they're baking!

6. Bake for 8–10 minutes, or until the edges are ever so lightly browned. Let them cool before you eat them, or they'll burn your tongue!

CAPTAIN VILLADS

He pronounces his name "Veelas," with a silent "d," but there's nothing silent about this pirate! A blind ship captain might seem like a strange choice to take us across the bay to get to Xadia, but we thought he wouldn't be able to tell that Rayla was an elf. Turns out, Villads doesn't need sight to see the truth!

ROLE: Sea captain

STRENGTHS AND SPECIAL SKILLS: Sailing the seas; navigating through storms; sharing his "good wisdom"

ACCESSORIES: His parrot, Berto

LIKES: The freedom of sailing on the open sea; his lovely boat-avoiding wife, Ruth

DISLIKES: Seagulls. His left eye was taken from him by a flock of them.

Villads's ship is called the <u>Ruthless</u>. As Villads said, "It's named after me dear wife, Ruth, who sadly, don't enjoy sailing."

Captain Villads really does have good wisdom! I'll never forget what he told me:

Life is like a river. You can't see too far ahead. Don't try to control where the river goes. There's one thing you can control — yourself. Once you know that, you'll be okay, no matter where the river takes you. —Rayla

Rayla HATES Water!

I was surprised that Rayla agreed to get on the pirate ship, because she <u>hates</u> water! I mean, she REALLY hates it. She gets sick whenever she's on a boat.

But that's what's amazing about Rayla — she pushes through her own fear if it means helping someone else. It was her idea to sail across the bay to get to Xadia faster. And then there was that time that she dove into the water to rescue Bait!

Into the Storm

During our sailing journey to Xadia, a storm struck — and an idea struck me. We were docked at a small island and I saw a windmill with a lightning rod on top. I thought if I was brave and faced the storm, I could make a connection to the Sky arcanum. If I could connect to the Sky arcanum, I'd be able to do magic on my own, without a primal stone.

More on arcana in the magic section!

Zym came with me. He loves the rain and wasn't afraid at all.

We climbed up to the top of the windmill . . .
but I chickened out before lightning struck.

I felt stupid for
risking my life —
and Zym's — but
Rayla made me feel
better, like she
always does.

XADIA

Now that we're in Xadia, I'm feeling a lot of stuff. My mom died here, so I should hate this place. But since I was little, I've always wanted to come here, to the land where magic is everywhere. And now I'm finally here!

It's beautiful. There are amazing plants and creatures that I've never seen before, and I want to sketch all of them! I also want to learn as much about magic as I can while we're here. But right now, there's no time. We need to get Zym to his mom as quickly as we can, and stop this war.

The BREACH and the

Getting into Xadia isn't easy! In fact, it's almost impossible. There are really only two ways to cross the border: the Breach and the Moonstone Path.

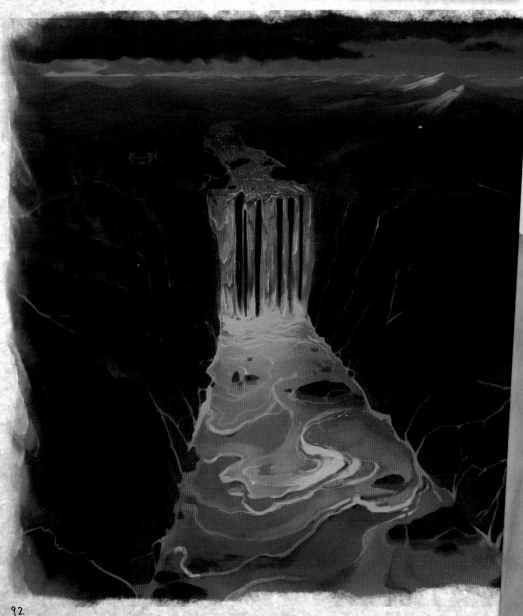

MOONSTONE PATH

THE BORDER (or what I like to call "The Lava River of Death") was created by magic when the continent was divided into the human world and the magical world. For some time, it seemed there was no possible way to cross the Border.

But humans eventually discovered a secret passage into Xadia, high above the river of lava. They named it **THE BREACH**. It's not like you can just walk right through into the other land, though. Aunt Amaya and her troops guard the human side and Sunfire elves guard the Xadian side.

Before I met Rayla, I thought the Breach was the only way into Xadia. But it turns out Moonshadow elves have their own secret way to cross the lava: the **MOONSTONE**

PATH. At this spot on the Border, the lava is covered with large flat stones. Most of the stones sink quickly if you step on them. But at night, the moon lights up runes — ancient symbols — on some of the stones. Those stones are safe to step on — if you're fast enough!

ELVES of XADIA

SUNFIRE ELVES harness the power of, well, the Sun and fire.

MOONSHADOW ELVES, like Rayla, connect to the powers of the Moon.

Rayla says that **STARTOUCH ELVES** are rarely seen.

I have to admit, walking into a land of elves made me a <u>little</u> nervous. I mean, I know Rayla isn't a bloodthirsty fiend, but I don't know much about other kinds of elves. So I asked Rayla and she's been explaining some things to me — like the fact that there are different types of elves that connect to the different primal sources. Maybe I'll get to meet them all someday!

TIDEBOUND ELVES are connected to the Ocean, but Rayla's never actually seen one. (Not a surprise, considering how much she hates the water!)

Only some **SKYWING ELVES** can fly! Fewer than one in ten are born with wings.

EARTHBLOOD ELVES are connected to trees and plants.

When we arrived in Xadia, we headed straight for Rayla's home in the land of the **MOONSHADOW ELVES.** I learned so much about Moonshadow elves there — and about Rayla, too.

Deep in the forest, Rayla's village is truly beautiful. Glowing moths flit around, and even the plants glow in the dark.

Rayla told me that they make the best Moonberry Surprise in her village, but she won't tell me what's in it!

If I told you, it wouldn't be a surprise! —Rayla

SILVERGROVE

If you're just walking in the forest, you won't see the village. You need a key for it to be revealed to you. It's not a metal key, though — it's a dance!

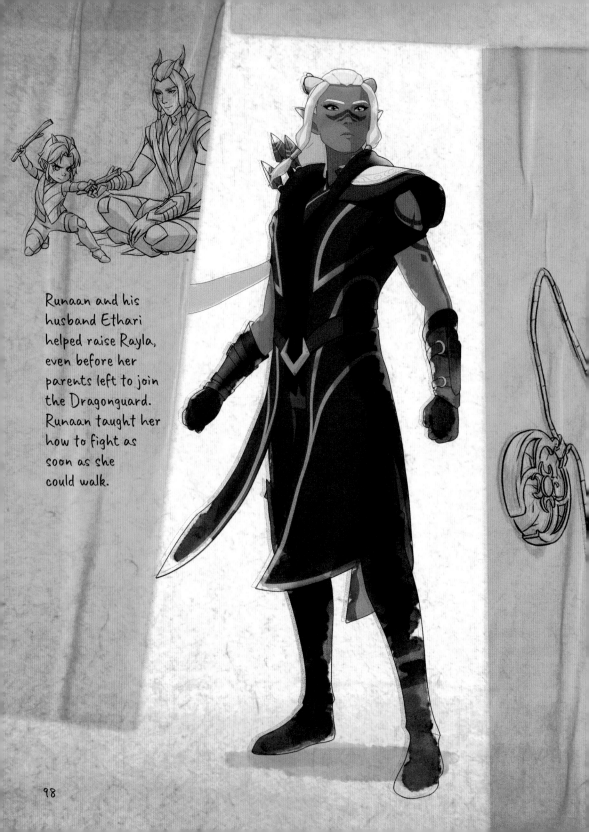

Runaan and his husband Ethari helped raise Rayla, even before her parents left to join the Dragonguard. Runaan taught her how to fight as soon as she could walk.

RUNAAN

This Moonshadow elf assassin led the mission to kill my stepdad and Ez. It looks like he didn't survive, and I know that's hard for Rayla. Besides being her teacher, Runaan was like a father to her. It would be so easy for me to hate him for killing King Harrow, but hate is what started all this in the first place . . .

ROLE: Leader of the Moonshadow elf assassins sent to Katolis

STRENGTHS/SPECIAL SKILLS: He was a master of archery, stealth, and speed.

WEAPONS/ACCESSORIES: Bow and arrows, which transform into dual blades; leather gauntlets; Moon opal pendant

LIKES: Ethari; Rayla; Moonberry Surprise; order

DISLIKES: Talking about his feelings; smiling; making small talk at gatherings

Moonshadow elves can transform into a super stealthy magical Moonshadow form when the moon is full.

Nobody could defeat Runaan in his Moonshadow form. But that night in the castle, Rayla was brave enough to try so that Ez and I could escape with the dragon egg.

99

ETHARI

Ethari is Runaan's husband, and he
also helped raise Rayla. He's a skilled
craftsman, specializing in elven weaponry.
Rayla says no one can craft a weapon
as light, elegant, strong, and clever as
Ethari can.

When an assassin is sent on a dangerous mission, Ethari enchants one of these lotus flowers for them. As long as the assassin lives and breathes, the flower floats.

The Assassins

Six Moonshadow assassins joined the mission to Katolis. Out of everyone, Rayla was the only one to make it home.

While Moonshadow elves are dark, cool, and quiet,
SUNFIRE ELVES are fiery and hot.

LUX AUREA

The Sunfire elves' city is made out of gold and stones that glitter in the sunlight.

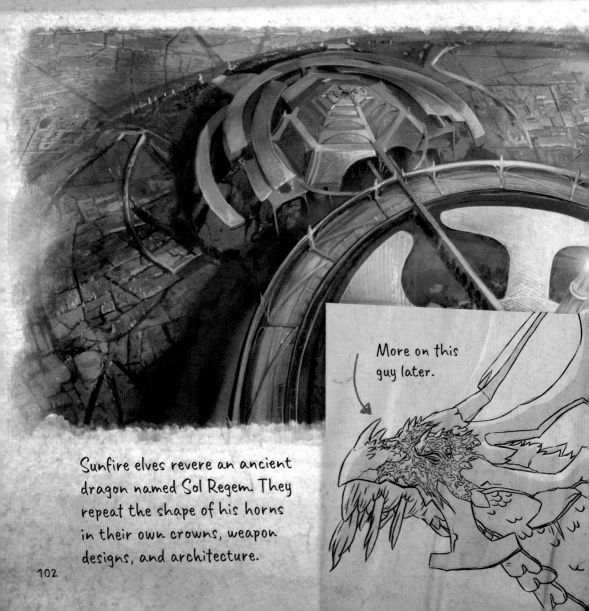

More on this guy later.

Sunfire elves revere an ancient dragon named Sol Regem. They repeat the shape of his horns in their own crowns, weapon designs, and architecture.

The SUNFORGE

Sunfire elves are powerful warriors known for creating powerful weapons. The **SUNFORGE** helps with that.

This magical hearth focuses light and primal magic from the Sun. Light concentrates within the orb and the disc rotates to aim the beam onto the forge below.

A **SUNFORGE BLADE** is a magical weapon that stays as hot as when it was forged. You need a special sheathe to carry it, because it will burn through anything!
Well . . . almost anything.
Rayla tried cutting her assassin's binding off with a Sunforge blade, but not even the searing metal could break the magic of the binding.

When they become angry, Sunfire elves can power up into HEAT-BEING MODE. Their skin glows with actual molten lava, and they become super-strong and can walk through fire!

Hey, nephew! You're right. Heat is one aspect of the Sun — but so is light. While it's rare, some Sunfire elves have a LIGHT-BEING MODE that allows them to heal others. Now you know!

—Aunt Amaya

Rayla says there is an elven saying, "Moon reflects Sun as death reflects life." So while Moonshadow and Sunfire elves are different, they are both powerful in their own way.

JANAI

Aunt Amaya says she never encountered a Sunfire elf who could best her in battle — until she met Janai.

ROLE: Sunfire knight

STRENGTHS/SPECIAL ABILITIES: She is an expert swordfighter who can power up into Heat-Being Mode.

WEAPONS/ACCESSORIES: Sunforge blade; golden armor; golden crown

LIKES: Fighting for her people; honorable warriors; spicy foods; all kinds of tea; "sweets that aren't too sweet"

DISLIKES: Cowardice; bad hats; "sweets that are too sweet, which is most sweets"; humans (That's kind of an elf trend, I guess. But it works both ways, too.)

The SUNFIRE QUEEN

She is Janai's older sister, and has a fierier temper than Janai does. While she is a fair ruler, she can be stubborn and will not always listen to her sister's advice.

ROLE: Queen of the Sunfire kingdom

STRENGTHS/SPECIAL SKILLS: She has protected Lux Aurea ever since the death of her grandmother.

WEAPONS/ ACCESSORIES: Scepter of Radiance; golden garments; golden crown; golden throne

LIKES: Letting the light of the Sun reveal the truth; sitting in stern judgment; dancing!

DISLIKES: Cowards who hide in the shadows; muggy weather

The ELVEN INTERPRETER

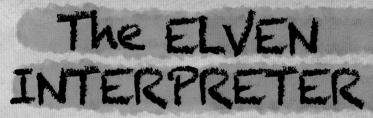

Aunt Amaya was impressed by this young elf, who was able to understand Katolis sign language. Their name is Kazi.

ROLE: Official interpreter for the Sunfire Queen

STRENGTHS/SPECIAL SKILLS: Top of their class in linguistics, although they wondered if the study of sign language should be called "finguistics" because you speak it with your fingers, and not your tongue.

ACCESSORIES: Extremely cool eyeglasses

LIKES: Daydreaming; hard work; studying. And learning new languages, which opens up the world to getting to know new people.

DISLIKES: Distractions; stress; oversleeping. Also, war; communication is a much more effective way of solving problems. (I couldn't agree more!)

The first
SKYWING ELF
I ever met was . . .

NYX

This impish elf told us her name is Naimi-Selari-Nykantia . . . but thankfully she goes by Nyx. She said she was working for the Dragon Queen and wanted us to give her Zym, but we refused.

ROLE: Guide across the Midnight Desert

STRENGTHS/SPECIAL SKILLS: Nyx was born with wings that allow her to fly.

WEAPONS/ACCESSORIES: Elven staff with boomerang blades attached to the end. She throws and catches the boomerangs with the staff!

LIKES: Her traveling companion, a huge creature called an ambler. She also secretly enjoys the smell of flatu-lillies!

DISLIKES: Getting caught; soulfang serpents; mushy stuff

THe MIDNIGHT

DESERT

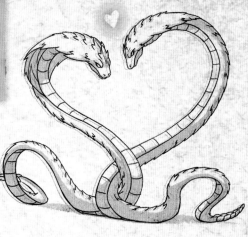

Nyx described this place as "hot, haunted, and horrifying," and she was right. The black sand soaks up the sun, so in the daytime the sand is super hot. At night, deadly **SOULFANG SERPENTS** come out. So in order to survive, you must reach the **CENTRAL OASIS** by sundown.

We could have gone around the Midnight Desert, but that would have taken an extra week — time we didn't have. So we allowed Nyx to be our guide and help us get across on an ambler, even though we didn't trust her.

I recently learned of an ancient mysterious figure named Aaravos. My letter from King Harrow explained that the Rune Cube is called "the Key of Aaravos" and said Aaravos was an elven archmage.

When I asked some of the elves I met in Xadia about him, most said they'd never heard the name or, if they had, they refused to talk about him at all. It's very strange!

As a new mage myself, I can't help but be curious about someone who has learned so much magic that they're called an "archmage." But why does everyone seem to hate and fear him so much?

One time, I found a very old book that had a picture of him in it, but the moment I looked at it, both the picture and his name disappeared as if they'd been soaked with ink! It was clear from his appearance that he was a Startouch elf. I'll redraw what I saw here:

I copied this text out of the book with Aaravos in it, but I have no idea what it means.

إلاريون ، جليس ثقيل
بكت بينما تحولت نجوم السماء إلى سواد ،
لقد ارتدوا أقنعتهم
أداروا ظهورهم ،
وتركوا الإريون لتموت.

إلاريون ، وقشرتها تصارع الموت ،
ذبلت و عنت في الظلام ،
حتى النجم الأخير
تواصل من بعيد
لمسته؛ حريق ، هدية ، شرارة.

إلاريون ، ببياضها الناصع ،
احتضنت اللهب الليلي الأسود الأعظم.
وعندما انحنت ،
أعلنت إيمانها ،
همس ، **"أرافوس"** ، اسمه.

إلاريون ، الطفلة ذو العيون السوداء ،
تنشر جذورها الملتوية بكل بعد
وبقوة الإنسان
اللتي اشتعلت
من أرافوس ، نجم منتصف الليل ، نجم منتصف الليل

إلاريون، بذور ترتجف
تستلقي على الأرض في ليلة جليدية.
وفي البرد
جذبت جذورها
تتحدى لدغة الشتاء القاتلة.

إلاريون ، وزهرتها المتفتحة ،
تخاف من الذبول والظلمة والموت.
لقد فتشت الظلام
عن شرارة
فاشتعلت عيون التنين الجائعة.

إلاريون ، اللقيطة الخائفة ،
أوصلت فروعها البيضاء نحو الليل ،
تسأل النجوم
لتلقي نورها
وتوقف نار التنين الهائجة.

إلاريون ، جليس ثقيل ،
بكت بينما تحولت نجوم السماء إلى سواد ،
لقد ارتدوا أقنعتهم
أداروا ظهورهم ،
وتركوا الإريون لتموت.

CREATURES of XADIA

I could spend a year just traveling around and sketching all of the amazing creatures I meet! I'm sure there are so many more to discover.

ARCHANGEL LUNARIS: These bird-sized moths have silvery wings and are tuned to the energy of the Moon and Moonshadow elves. Soren tried to use one to track down Runaan's assassin crew before they attacked Katolis.

BANTHER: These creatures are native to Katolis, but they sure look magical to me. I'm guessing they roamed the whole land before it was split in two.

ADORABURR: They're adorable, and they stick together like burrs — get it? (I love words like that!) I can't get over how cute they are, and they come in every color of the rainbow!

It's a good look for me, isn't it?

AMBLER: I don't think I've ever seen a creature as big as this before! We rode on one of these giant, gentle beasts to safely cross the Midnight Desert.

MOONSHADOW & SUNFIRE MOUNTS:

I kind of think of these mounts as horses for elves. They're not horses, but they are swift, strong, and steady — and magical.

This is a MOONSTRIDER.

This one's called a SHADOWPAW.

This is a TWIN-TAILED INFERNO-TOOTH TIGER . . . but most folks just call them "hotcats."

SUNBIRDS: These birds are so beautiful when they fly across the sky.

SOULFANG SERPENT: Not every creature in Xadia is cute and cuddly. Soulfang serpents literally suck the souls out of their prey, leaving them lifeless husks. We had a couple close encounters with soulfang serpents in the Midnight Desert.

MAGMA TITAN: The magma titan was a magnificent creature, but it'll always remind me of my mother's death and the start of this whole war. The people of Katolis were starving. Lord Viren convinced my stepdad that the heart of a magma titan could be used in a dark magic spell to grow food. My mom argued that it was wrong to kill a thinking, feeling creature, but King Harrow wouldn't listen. They slayed the magma titan and used its heart to save thousands of human lives. Then Thunder killed my mother in revenge . . . then Lord Viren and Harrow killed Thunder . . . and now here we are.

DRAGONS

# of XADIA

Dragons live peacefully in Xadia, alongside the elves. I am learning more about dragons every day. Here's a list of what I know so far:

- Dragons are the most **POWERFUL** creatures in the world.

- All dragons are **CONNECTED** to the six primal sources — the Moon, the Sun, the Sky, the Stars, the Ocean, and the Earth. Dragons who have extra-deep connections to the primal sources are called **ARCHDRAGONS**. They're massively huge and powerful. (Zym's dad was an archdragon, and Zym will be one someday, too.)

- Other dragon types are smaller than the archdragons, but they still have primal source connections. For example, a **CLOUD WYVERN** is a type of Sky dragon, but is not as big or as powerful as Zym's dad was.

- Dragons are complex, **INTELLIGENT** beings, just like humans and elves. Some of them live alone, and some live in groups.

- They can **SPEAK**.

- Dragons live for a very, very, very **LONG TIME**.

- There aren't a whole lot of dragons, because it's very rare that a dragon egg is born. For example, the Dragon Queen only **LAYS AN EGG** once every few centuries!

PYRRAH

This Fire dragon is the second dragon I ever met, after Zym. Ez told me her name was Pyrrah. She was flying near a human village when Soren, Claudia, and some soldiers decided to attack.

Rayla faced them all to save the dragon, but I couldn't let Rayla do it on her own. I used a dark magic spell I had seen Claudia do to free the dragon from her chains. Maybe that was dangerous, but I don't regret it. I know that helping Pyrrah was the right thing to do.

AVIZANDUM
The Dragon King

The humans called him Thunder, because his voice shook the earth and sky, but his real name was Avizandum. He was Zym's dad, and he was an archdragon of Sky. King Harrow and Lord Viren killed him to avenge the death of my mom.

ROLE: Former King of the Dragons; guardian of the border of Xadia

STRENGTHS AND SPECIAL SKILLS: He could see a thousand miles to detect any threats to the border. He could transform his body into lightning and travel to meet a human threat in an instant. Then he could frighten or destroy them with the force of thunder.

WEAKNESS: He was most vulnerable when protecting his precious heir.

He was so powerful that all the other dragons — and all the elves, too — accepted him as their king. It's tough to imagine cute little Zym turning into such a powerful creature!

The day Lord Viren and my stepdad set out to kill Avizandum just happened to be the day the dragon egg was born. Harrow and Lord Viren used dark magic to turn him into **LIFELESS STONE** while he was reaching toward the Dragon Queen and their precious egg. His form still stares at the Storm Spire to this day.

When I think about what happened, it makes me sad
and angry and confused all at the same time. How
am I supposed to feel? Happy that we got revenge?
Or maybe regretful because that was Zym's dad?
Mainly, I feel so sorry that this all happened . . .

123

SOL REGEM

Sol Regem is an archdragon of Sun. Before Avizandum was king, Sol Regem ruled Xadia. He still guards a canyon pass near the border, but he relies on scent and sound to detect intruders because he is now blind.

ROLE: He was King of the Dragons when the first war with humans began.

STRENGTHS AND SPECIAL SKILLS:
Sol Regem connects to the Sun primal source, and can harness that power into massively destructive fiery blasts.

WEAKNESS: His hatred of humans and dark magic has twisted him into an angry dragon.

When he was King of the Dragons, Sol Regem was powerful, gleaming, and proud. The Sunfire elves worshipped him. But a long time ago, when the first wars between the human world and Xadia began, a powerful dark mage challenged him. Sol Regem destroyed the dark mage, but was blinded in the process. Rayla says he's been a symbol of rage and bitterness ever since.

Getting Zym safely past Sol Regem wasn't easy, but Rayla had some good advice for us: "The secret of stealth is that you don't have to be invisible. You just have to be invisible to your enemy's senses."

ZUBEIA
The Dragon Queen

Zubeia is the Dragon Queen, Zym's mom. When King Harrow and Lord Viren killed Thunder — I mean, Avizandum — Lord Viren made it look like he had destroyed Zym's egg. Zubeia must have been heartbroken!

I don't know much about her. I don't know if she's as powerful as the king was — or even more powerful. I don't know if she'll agree to stop the war just because we bring Zym back to her.

But I know we have to try. Whatever happens, Zym needs to be with his mom. Ez, Rayla, and I might not have parents anymore, but we have people and elves around us who are our family. And Zym — Zym still has us. But he needs his dragon family, too. He needs his mom.

I just hope we get to her in time!

The STORM

This is it – where our whole journey has been headed. The highest point in Xadia, the Storm Spire is where the dragon egg was born and watched over by elven guards until Lord Viren stole it. Now it's where Zym's mother is waiting for us to return her son.

the Dragonguard

Zym's parents must have been so happy when his egg was born!

SPIRE

We learned the hard way that it gets
harder to breathe the higher you go. On the way up, there is an archway
that says, "Prepare to draw your last breath," in Elven. That sounded pretty
hopeless. But Ez figured out the secret. You have to <u>literally</u> draw breath, by
drawing a magical rune. Phew!

REX IGNEOUS

Rayla told me that Rex Igneous is an archdragon of Earth. Neither of us have met him, and it's possible we never will, since he lives deep beneath a mountain and only emerges aboveground every hundred years or so. But he seems so intriguing! She described him to me and I drew him here:

When I asked her if I got my drawing anywhere close, she shrugged and told me she's never met the big guy in person — but she'll keep me posted if he comes up for some fresh air any time in the next century.

Rumor has it that Rex Igneous can sometimes be appeased if he is presented with extraordinary food that he has never tried before. Dragons are weird. And awesome.

MAGIC!

I know that this journey is about bringing Zym back to his mom, but for me, it's about something else, too: becoming a mage.

I didn't even know I could be a mage until the night I met Rayla — the night the Moonshadow elf assassins attacked the castle. I used Claudia's Sky primal stone to cast a spell, and it felt <u>amazing</u>. I could feel the magic throughout my whole body. At that moment, I knew magic was my destiny.

I'm going to dedicate myself to becoming the best mage I can be. So I'm writing down everything I learn. So far, I've learned a lot from Rayla, Lujanne, and Claudia — plus what I've learned on my own. I've taken some risks and I've made some mistakes, but I know that every day I'm getting closer to reaching my goal!

PRIMAL MAGIC

Any time you perform magic, you are connecting to one of the six **PRIMAL SOURCES** of nature. This magical energy is infused in everything in Xadia. It is stronger in different places and at different times.

In Xadia, all creatures are born connected to a primal source. Sunfire elves are born connected to the Sun. An archangel lunaris moth is born connected to the Moon. Xadian creatures have a piece of the primal source magic in them, and that's called the **ARCANUM**.

But everyone says that humans <u>aren't</u> born connected to a primal source. (That's why we need primal stones to perform magic. And it's why humans figured out how to use dark magic.)

But . . . I think they're wrong. I can feel the pull of magic inside me. I think I can learn how to connect to the Sky arcanum, and I'm going to try.

On the following pages is everything I know so far about the magic of each primal source. I'm going to keep adding to these pages as I learn more!

Rayla drew the runes for me that represent each primal source:

the Sun

the Moon

the Sky

the Stars

the Ocean

the Earth

MOON Magic

Thanks to Rayla and Lujanne, I know a little more about Moon magic than any other kind.

TO SUM IT UP: Moon magic is all about the spirit and energy of the Moon, including an "out of this world" feeling. That's why a lot of Moon magic has to do with illusions. Moon magic is also cyclical in its strength; it gets weaker or stronger depending on the phase of the moon. The Moon arcanum is "understanding the relationship between appearance and reality," which is why Lujanne, the Moon mage who guards the Moon Nexus on the Cursed Caldera, is so good at illusions.

WHEN THE MAGIC IS STRONGEST:
During a full moon

MOON MAGIC I'VE SEEN:
Lujanne's illusions; Rayla's assassin's binding; the Moonstone Path; Ethari's enchanted lotus flowers

As I learn more about each kind of magic, I'm going to jot down words that remind me of it. Here are some words for Moon magic:

Illusion
Love
Charm
Private
Deep
Secrets

Manipulation
Death
Reflection
Appearances
Duality

SKY Magic

This is the primal source I feel most connected to. If I am going to connect to an arcanum, it's going to be the Sky arcanum.

TO SUM IT UP: I've heard some people refer to Sky magic as "the weather magic," but it's so much more than that. Sky magic draws on the vastness of the Sky and the energy and movement of the winds. Oh. And lightning. Lightning is kind of a big deal in Sky magic. And flying!

WHEN THE MAGIC IS STRONGEST: During a storm

SKY MAGIC I HAVE SEEN: The Aspiro spell, which creates wind; the Fulminis spell, which creates lightning; and I've seen Nyx, a Skywing elf, fly.

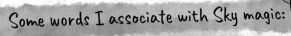

Some words I associate with Sky magic:

Lightness
Quickness
Agility
Cleverness
Vision
Potential
Freedom
Perspective

SUN Magic

Most of what I know about Sun magic is from the Sunfire elves. I have to admit, the fiery heat of Sun magic is pretty intense. It scares me a little bit!

TO SUM IT UP: Sun magic draws from the heat and energy of the Sun. It can be life-giving (think how sunlight helps plants grow) or oppressive and destructive (think how much a sunburn hurts). A lot of Sun spells involve fire, which is both awesome and scary. Sun mages project a very positive energy overall, though; they believe their mission is to bring more light and hope into the world.

WHEN THE MAGIC IS STRONGEST:
When the sun is highest

SUN MAGIC I HAVE SEEN: When we first arrived in Ellis's village, we saw a mercenary fighting in the street using a Sunforge blade. It was just as powerful as Rayla told us — but not powerful enough to break her assassin's binding.

Words for Sun magic:

Energy	Teaching	Truth
Fury	Warmth	Honesty
Intensity	Charisma	Leadership
Optimism	Revealing	Guiding light

EARTH Magic

Rayla hasn't told me much about Earth magic. But when I need to disguise myself as an elf in Xadia, an Earthblood elf is my go-to disguise!

TO SUM IT UP: Earth magic draws on the power and energy of the land itself. Earth magic has two main types: 1) magic relating to stone, minerals, crystals, and gems; and 2) druidic magic relating to trees, plants, nature, animals, and the like.

WHEN THE MAGIC IS STRONGEST:
When you're deep underground

EARTH MAGIC I HAVE SEEN:
Nothing yet, but I wonder if all of those amazing plants I saw in the Xadian forest are connected to the Earth primal source?

Here are some plants I remember:

The melodaisy plays music. And this one shoots out stinky gas! It's called a flatu-lily, or a peri-stinkle, but its most common name is fart flower. Yeah, that's right.

Words that seem Earth magic-y to me:

Strength	Patience
Endurance	Healing
Stubbornness	Growth
Deep history	Balance

OCEAN Magic

This is probably the primal source I know the least about right now. Katolis Castle is far from the ocean. But from what Lujanne told me, any kind of water magic is connected to the Ocean primal source. I think that means that Ocean magic can be found in any river or stream.

TO SUM IT UP: Ocean magic draws on the depth and power of the oceans and tides. It also includes ice magic, like freezing spells. I've been wondering, can Ocean mages breathe underwater? (That would have come in handy when Ezran dove into the water to retrieve the dragon egg after it fell through the ice!)

WHEN THE MAGIC IS STRONGEST: At high tide

OCEAN MAGIC I HAVE SEEN: Nothing yet, though we were almost eaten by a river monster on our way to Xadia. Maybe that creature was magical?

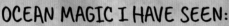

Words that seem like they'd be related to Ocean magic:

Flexibility

Transformation

Flow

Surface level vs. depth

Navigation

Awareness

STAR Magic

Rayla tells me that Star magic might be the most powerful magic there is. It's very mysterious, and not much is known about it. Probably because the stars are so far away . . .

TO SUM IT UP: Star magic is sometimes called "celestial magic" or "cosmic magic." It draws on the vast and timeless power of the cosmos. Honestly, I've heard that Star magic can be a little . . . "out there," sort of hard to understand. Star mages are extremely rare — only one Star mage may be born in generations.

WHEN THE MAGIC IS STRONGEST: ???

STAR MAGIC I HAVE SEEN: I do have one connection to Star magic: the Rune Cube I found in the Banther Lodge. I have more notes on that coming up, because I am discovering new things about it all the time!

Some words that might be related to Star magic:

Vision
Truth

Mysterious
Timeless
Reality-altering

Intelligence
Otherworldly
Destiny
Wishes

The RUNE CUBE

Somehow, I feel like me having this cube is destiny. I remember seeing it at the Banther Lodge when I was a kid and thinking it was a toy.

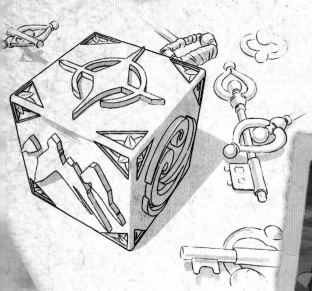

But when Rayla drew the primal source runes for me, I recognized them right away. I had this feeling that we needed to go to the Banther Lodge to get it, and we did.

Later, I found out that King Harrow wanted me to have it. That's more than a coincidence, isn't it? There's something really special about this cube, but I need to know more about it. Here's what I know so far:

- It belonged to a **POWERFUL ELVEN WIZARD** named Aaravos.

- It's called the **KEY OF AARAVOS**, and it's supposed to unlock something important, but what?

- When I hold it near something that contains magic, the **CORRESPONDING RUNE GLOWS.** For example, if I hold it near Bait, the Sun rune glows, because glow toads are connected to the Sun primal source.

- I've been noticing that something interesting happens whenever I roll the cube on the ground: It leaves marks pointing in the same direction every time. Once we got to Xadia, the marks started getting longer, but still pointed in the same direction. Is the cube **BEING PULLED SOMEWHERE?**

PRIMAL STONES

One thing I've learned in Xadia is that even though magic is everywhere, and is everything, I need to be near natural primal energy to cast a spell. It's easy to perform Sky magic in a storm, because that natural primal energy is all around me.

But what if you're an Ocean mage, and you're stuck in the middle of a desert? That's where primal stones come in. A really long time ago, mages used rituals to capture primal energy and contain it inside powerful orbs. So if that Ocean mage had an Ocean primal stone, she could cast her magic anywhere in the world, whether she was near the ocean or not.

I asked Rayla why humans didn't just use primal stones instead of turning to dark magic, and she said it's because primal stones are extremely rare. The magic used to make them has been forgotten.

I still feel kind of bad about breaking the Sky primal stone that I took from Claudia. I know it can never be replaced. It meant a lot to me, because that stone helped me understand that I'm a mage. It helped me connect to magic.

But when Zym was dying inside his dragon egg, Lujanne told us that he had to hatch to survive. And he needed a storm to hatch. I knew what I needed to do. I smashed the Sky primal stone and released the storm inside. It wasn't an easy decision — but I know saving Zym was the right thing to do.

RUNE MAGIC

Connecting to a primal source — in nature or with a primal stone — is just the first step in performing a spell. Once you have attracted the energy, you need to **FOCUS IT**, and then **RELEASE IT**.

To focus primal energy, you **TRACE A RUNE** in the air with your finger. I learned this from Claudia. Then, you have to release the spell by saying the right **DRACONIC WORD** — that's a word in the language of the dragons.

Claudia has spent years studying all kinds of runes and Draconic words. The only spells I know, I know because I've seen her do them. I don't know if I'll ever be as good a mage as Claudia is, but I'll try!

My First Spell:
ASPIRO

2

Aspiro is a Sky magic spell. I saw Claudia do it once. When Rayla, Ez, and I discovered that Lord Viren was keeping the dragon egg hidden, Claudia tried to stop us from taking it. I took her Sky primal stone from her, but she sent dark magic wolves made of smoke after us. I held the stone in my hand, traced the rune, and said, "Aspiro!" Then I blew the smoke wolves away and we escaped.

Aspiro is a very handy spell to know!
I've used it a few times since then:

- When we got caught in an avalanche, I used Aspiro to blow back the snow.

- I helped Zym finally take flight so he could block the sun, allowing us to cross the border on the Moonstone Path.

- I blew my scarf (and my scent!) away from Sol Regem when we were trying to get past him into Xadia.

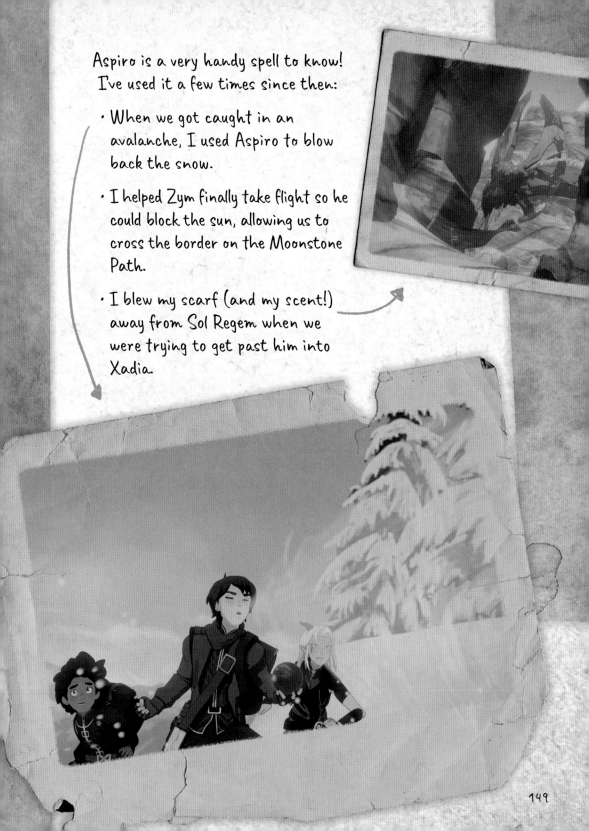

My Second Spell:
FULMINIS

This is a really cool spell that lets you cast actual lightning bolts! Claudia tried to aim one at Rayla when we were escaping the castle with the dragon egg, but I stopped her. Later, I tried to practice the spell, but I forgot the Draconic word. I almost fried myself! I tossed the primal stone to stop the spell. From now on, I'll never start a spell unless I know how to finish it!

It was Rayla who remembered the Draconic word for lightning: Fulminis. Once I knew that, I started using Fulminis for real. I used it to stop a giant leech from attacking us on the Cursed Caldera.

Of course, now that I've destroyed the Sky primal stone, I'll never be able to perform Fulminis or Aspiro again. Not unless I find a way to connect to the Sky arcanum. I know I can do it! I have to believe I can. Because if I'm not a mage, then who am I?

USING DARK MAGIC

It's so cute that you're keeping a little spellbook of your own, Callum! I bet you'll be a great mage, but I don't understand why you're so against using dark magic. Humans weren't born with magic, like all those snooty elves were; we were born with nothing. But we still learned how to do amazing things! That's what dark magic is really all about.

Think of dark magic as a sort of handy shortcut. Since we don't have our own magic, we have to take it from other creatures. Everybody squashes bugs we don't like, right? All humans do it. So what's wrong with me squashing an emberback spider so I can use its magical energy to create a fireball? That fireball could save someone's life in a battle – a human life. Isn't a human life more valuable than a spider's life? (I happen to believe that even the life of the jerkiest human is worth more than the life of a saint among bugs.)

Dark magic isn't creepy or wrong; think of it as the seventh source, which just happens to be the only one we humans can use easily. Get over your fear of dark magic, Callum, and you'll be a really great mage some day!

– Claudia

PS - Did you know there are some little dark magic spells you can use to permanently enchant your fingers and hands to do neat tricks? This is how I can use my hand as a light, or flick a candle on with a snap.

I know Claudia means well (and a hand-light is pretty cool), but I don't think she's telling the whole truth. Humans kill more than spiders for their dark magic spells. They kill beautiful creatures, like unicorns and phoenixes. And my mom always said that dark magic changes the mage using it . . . it corrupts them and makes them evil. I hope that doesn't happen to Claudia! I know that deep down her heart is good.

Here are some dark magic spells, Callum, so you can see how they work. Dark magic doesn't use Draconic language. Instead, it uses human words spoken backward. It's not hard once you get the hang of it! But please don't try to do any of these on your own. You need somebody to teach you how to do them safely; you need a dark mage buddy — me!

LIGHTING A FIRE

This one is really useful! Crush an emberback spider and chant backward, "Leaping skipping flames." It will create a small flame that jumps between any targets you think about when you are saying the spell.

SILENCE SPELL

Using the mummified paw of a Xadian singing-weasel (altos work best, but soprano or tenor weasels will work in a pinch), chant backward, "Steal the voice." A magic light will slide down your target's throat and prevent them from speaking.

Lord Viren used this one on me!

TRACKING SPELL

This one's a little more advanced: First, you need a piece of hair or toenail from the person you're tracking. Then you need a jar of magic wisps. When you get both, climb to the top of the highest mountain in the land. Light the hair on fire and chant backward, "Fuse your essence," to create a magical purple flame. Infuse the wisps with the purple flame, and then chant, "Seek (name of the person you're tracking)," and launch the wisps in the direction of your target.

SMOKE WOLVES

For this one, sprinkle the ashes of Xadian wolves on a "Shadowlife Candle" (made from the blood of a Moon phoenix mixed with earwax from a dragon). Then chant backward, "Ash of fallen, rise again smoky seekers," and send the wolves to do your bidding. (Tip: This can be used with ashes of other things, not just wolves.)

See what I mean? Ashes of wolves and blood of a phoenix. That's <u>cruel!</u>

SNAKE CHAINS

I use my snake bracelets for this one. I don't know exactly how the bracelets were originally crafted, but, like the weasel paws, they are enchanted with dark magic. If I chant backward, "Slithering steel, bind them," the bracelets turn back into snakes, then transform into chains to bind my enemies.

From DARKNESS to LIGHT

I never thought I'd use dark magic. Never. But when Rayla tried to protect the Fire dragon, I had to help her. I remembered Claudia's snake chain spell — if Claudia could bind her enemies, maybe I could <u>un</u>bind them. I took her spellbook when she wasn't looking, and I found the rattle from a magical snake in her bag. Then I chanted the spell backward: "Slithering steel, unbind!"

I saved the dragon, and Rayla. But I paid a price. I felt sick. Like I had been poisoned or something. Then I fell asleep, and I had a really strange vision. First, I had this argument with . . . myself. Like, an evil version of me. About whether it's right to do dark magic or not.

Then Captain Villads appeared on his boat. We sailed on a stormy sea. "Be like the wind!" he told me, and suddenly I became the boat's sail! Then the vision changed . . . and I was steering the ship. Some weird things happened, and the ship smashed into pieces. I started to sink into the water, deeper . . . and deeper.

Then I heard my mom's voice . . . telling me to breathe. "To know something truly and deeply, you must know it with your head, hand, and heart. Mind, body, and spirit," she told me.

When I woke up, I saw that Rayla had been watching over me the whole time. That made me happy. And something else made me happy, too. I finally understood the Sky arcanum!

2 I AM THE WING! 3

Understanding the Sky arcanum wasn't about learning one thing — it was about all the things. They just had to come together. I finally get it. The whole world is like a giant primal stone, and we're in it! I'm _inside_ Sky magic, but it's also in me, with every breath I take.

I kept thinking about birds, and sails, and how they connect to the wind, and I thought I had to find my wings. But that's just it. I don't need wings. I _am_ the wing.

So I stepped into the breeze. I closed my eyes.
I breathed. I breathed some more. And then
I traced the rune and said the word: "Aspiro."
And I did it! I created wind! Without a primal
stone, and without using dark magic.

It's official now.

I'M A MAGE!!! Uh, I mean . . . I'm a mage.

My tip to anyone trying to learn something hard: Sometimes
there can be so much that it feels overwhelming, frustrating,
and impossible. My advice is to try to be patient, and breathe,
and trust that eventually you will get it!

Connecting to the Sky arcanum was awesome. Amazing. But it's not the most important thing. The most important thing is to get Zym back to his mom.

When I look at him, I see more than a cute little dragon. I see hope. Hope for the future. Because if we succeed — when we succeed — we'll bring peace to the human world and to Xadia. I know that so many generations before us fell into the traps of mistrust, and eventually violence and war. But I believe we can be different, and build a future of love.

Cheesy, right?

Not cheesy at all, Callum. Love is magic!
— Rayla